Daleeia's

OH NO, Second Grade!

Authors
Lakisha Tucker
Daleeia Tucker

Illustrator
Sameer Kassar

Edited By Sonya McTillman

Copyright @ 2020

ISBN 978-1-7322138-2-1

Dedication Page

Kiran, Daleeia, and Ella, you are my biggest motivational push. You keep me in a place of wanting to do more, wanting to be a better parent. Don't ever stop dreaming!!!

Daleeia, you've been a shining star from the moment you were conceived, you have grown into everything I could have ever hoped or imagined.

Love Mom

Thank you Jesus for never taking your hands off me!

Chapter One
Preparation for Second Grade

Oh no! Second grade!
I didn't know what to expect,
but just from what I'd heard,
I was an absolute wreck.

I was petrified of the stories
and rumbles of how hard it
would be.
We did what most families do.
We were busy like worker
bees, getting ready for
the first day of school.

We put my name on all my supplies and loaded them into my backpack, which was really cool.

9

It was the next morning and
Mom, came in to wake me up,
but my face was stuck.
Stuck to the pillow with fear.
Oh no, that dreaded day
could not be here!

I could hear mom's footsteps,
they sounded like a loud buck.

She called again with "It's time
to get up!" She was excited, but
I felt like yuck.

I tried to drag myself out of bed.
One leg, then two.

I found myself not knowing
what to do.
I stretched and I yawned,
 I even gave a loud,
"Aaaaaaachoo!"

After the loud sneeze
I bent my knees
to stand up, grabbed
my shorts and my top.
I could hear mom saying,
"Chop chop!"

She said, "We have to leave
soon if you want to be on time."
Being on time was my last
concern,
I was worried about
what I would learn!
And most of all, would I have
fun?

Would my teacher be nice like sugar and spice? Or would he be like an explosive device?

Would he yell and scream
and be really mean?
Or would he be every
student's dream?

Chapter Two
Getting up, and moving forward

As we drove to school mom reminded me to be courteous and nice.
And most of all not to do anything that would embarrass her. I could clearly hear her say, "You don't just represent you. You represent us too."

SCHOOL BUS

We parked the car for me to walk in.
It was anything but calm.
It seemed like a zoo!
There were moms, dads,
sisters and brothers too.

SCHOOL

29

The hallway never seemed
to end. We walked by class
after class after class,
as if we were watching
an hourglass.

I didn't know what happened, first there was a big SPLAT. I found my face FLAT against the wall, oh boy was it a great fall.

My book bag flew up in the air, my lunch box followed it somewhere.

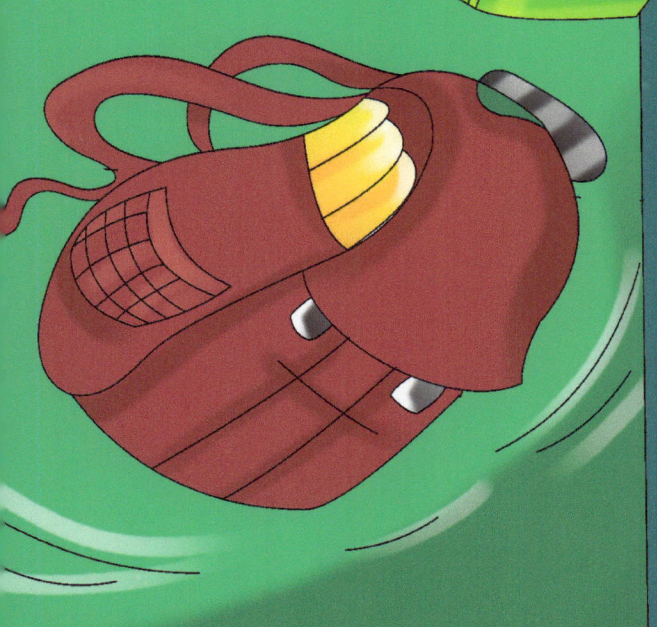

Everyone sprinted to help me up. Mom on the left, Dad on the right,
they grabbed my arms oh so tight.

I flung my things on my back.
I already thought the first
day was whack.

37

Chapter Three
Nothing is too hard

The teacher was standing
at the door waiting
for students to enter the room.
As I entered the door
I felt a magnetic boom!

I looked to the left, then to the right to see what happened. It was like the whole class was clapping.

I thought, had I entered the wrong class?
Was I really in the right space?
I remember hearing mom say something about the race.

I gazed at her face and could hear her say, "Remember Daleeia, the race is not given to the swift or to the strong, but to the one that endures until the end."

45

Maybe, just maybe
second grade could begin and
I could make some new friends.
Perhaps I will never know
how something will end
until I try it for myself.

So second grade here I come.
I'm putting my fear on the shelf,
picking up my faith and my
pride.
Watch out for my stride!

My friends and I are walking in confidence. We are going to love math, social studies, reading and science.

51

BEEP, BEEP, BEEP.

Wait. Is that my alarm?
You must be pulling my arm!

Tring tring

53

I was fast asleep this entire
time!
Now, I can climb out of bed
and start second grade
in a great way instead.

The End

About the Author

Rev Lakisha L. Tucker B.A., B.S., M. S

Lakisha Tucker is an Educator, Licensed Substance Abuse and Addiction Counselor (LCAS-A), and a Licensed Minister of the Gospel of Jesus Christ. Lakisha believes that it is her passion to work with youth and their families. Lakisha comes from a long line of educators and it was important to her to continue to carry the torch. She believes that all children can go from students to scholars within their own abilities. She also understands the struggle that families face when addiction and abuse comes into play.

She was born and raised in Greensboro NC, and reared in a single parent home along with her sister. Lakisha is a mother, wife, sister and friend. Lakisha learned early about hard work, determination, ethics, resilience, and tenacity. Lakisha graduated from Southeast Guilford High School in 1992. She matriculated to North Carolina A&T State University (NCA&T SU) where she earned a degree in Psychology. She had a thirst for education and went back to obtain a degree in Special Education in 2004 (also from NC A&T SU). With the passion to serve people and help them fulfill their life's purpose she received her Master's in Mental Health Counseling in 2013.

It was after a negative situation at her daughter's school that she became an author, writing her first children's book I Just Want to be Me! She went on to write a memoir, A Sun's Journey and a journal Learning to Thrive through Tough Transitions. She is currently in the final stages of her next book. She has also been given the gift of poetry and been called the Author Extraordinaire. Lakisha has a blog on wordpress.com along with a popular story telling corner that she created during the pandemic "Kisha's Korner."